A Note to Parents

For many children, learning math is difficult and "I hate math!" is their first response — to which many parents silently add "Me, too!" Children often see adults comfortably reading and writing, but they rarely have such models for mathematics. And math fear can be catching!

The easy-to-read stories in this **Hello Reader! Math** series were written to give children a positive introduction to mathematics, and parents a pleasurable re-acquaintance with a subject that is important to everyone's life. **Hello Reader! Math** stories make mathematical ideas accessible, interesting, and fun for children. The activities and suggestions at the end of each book provide parents with a hands-on approach to help children develop mathematical interest and confidence.

Enjoy the mathematics!
• Give your child a chance to retell the story. The more familiar children are with the story, the more they will understand its mathematical concepts.
• Use the colorful illustrations to help children "hear and see" the math at work in the story.
• Treat the math activities as games to be played for fun. Follow your child's lead. Spend time on those activities that engage your child's interest and curiosity.
• Activities, especially ones using physical materials, help make abstract mathematical ideas concrete.

Learning is a messy process. Learning about math calls for children to become immersed in lively experiences that help them make sense of mathematical concepts and symbols.

Although learning about numbers is basic to math, other ideas, such as identifying shapes and patterns, measuring, collecting and interpreting data, reasoning logically, and thinking about chance, are also important. By reading these stories and having fun with the activities, you will help your child enthusiastically say "**Hello, math**," instead of "I hate math."

—Marilyn Burns
National Mathematics Educator
Author of *The I Hate Mathematics! Book*

For Sarah Jackson
— J.R.

Copyright © 1998 by Scholastic Inc.
The activities on pages 43-48 copyright © 1998 by Marilyn Burns.
All rights reserved. Published by Scholastic Inc.
SCHOLASTIC, HELLO READER! and CARTWHEEL BOOKS
and associated logos are trademarks and/or registered trademarks of Scholastic Inc.

Library of Congress Cataloging-in-Publication Data

Rocklin, Joanne.
  The case of the shrunken allowance / by Joanne Rocklin;
illustrated by Cornelius Van Wright & Ying-Hwa Hu; math activities
by Marilyn Burns.
    p.   cm, — (Hello reader! Math. Level 4)
  Summary: Mike and his friends try to figure out why the money in his
allowance jar appears to be shrinking. Includes related math activities.
  ISBN 0-590-12006-9
  [1. Money—Fiction.   2. Measurements—Fiction.]   I. Van Wright,
Cornelius, ill.   II. Hu, Ying-Hwa, ill.   III. Burns, Marilyn
. IV. Title. V. Series
PZ7.R59Cau 1999
[Fic]—DC21   97-43664
                                                                      CIP
                                                                       AC

12 11 10 9 8 7 6 5 4 3   01 02 03 04

Printed in the U.S.A.   24
First printing, November 1998

THE CASE OF THE $HRUNKEN ALLOWANCE

by Joanne Rocklin
Illustrated by Cornelius Van Wright and Ying-Hwa Hu
Math Activities by Marilyn Burns

Hello Reader! Math — Level 4

SCHOLASTIC INC.
Cartwheel ·B·O·O·K·S·®
New York Toronto London Auckland Sydney

Chapter One: Something Terrible

"Hurry up!" said Maria.
"Why?" asked Mike.
"We have lots of time
until the big game."
Maria checked her watch.

"We are on a tight schedule," she said.
"12:00 P.M. to 12:30 P.M. We go home and eat lunch.

12:30 P.M. to 12:45 P.M. We walk to the park.

12:45 P.M. to 1:00 P.M. We practice hitting balls.

1:00 P.M. to 2:00 P.M. We win our game!"

"Win that game!" said Mike.

"*PSST! PSST!*"
"What was that?" asked Maria.
"What was what?" asked Mike.
"I heard something!" Maria said.
"*PSST!* Over here!" a voice called.
"Behind the tree!"

Mike and Maria looked behind the tree.
"Oh, it's you," said Maria.
"Hi, P.B." said Mike.

P.B. was wearing a big hat.
He was eating a peanut butter sandwich.
"Why are you wearing that silly hat?" asked
Maria.
"This is my spy hat," answered P.B. "I am in
disguise. I guess it's not a very good disguise."
"You are right," said Mike. "We knew
it was you."
"Who else eats so many peanut butter
sandwiches?" asked Maria.

"Have one," said P.B.
"Have some fruit punch, too."
"We don't have time," said Maria.
"We are on a tight schedule."
"Let's eat lunch with P.B.,"
said Mike. "We'll save time that way."
"You're right," said Maria.

"You can help me spy," said P.B.
"I have an important mystery to solve."
"What mystery?" asked Maria.
"See that peanut butter jar
in the window?" asked P.B.
"Watch that jar very carefully."

Maria and Mike looked at the jar
in the window.
"Why are we spying on
a jar of peanut butter?" asked Mike.
"We are *not* spying on a jar
of peanut butter!" P.B. answered.
"But you just said—" said Maria.
"You were not listening," said P.B.
"Take a closer look."

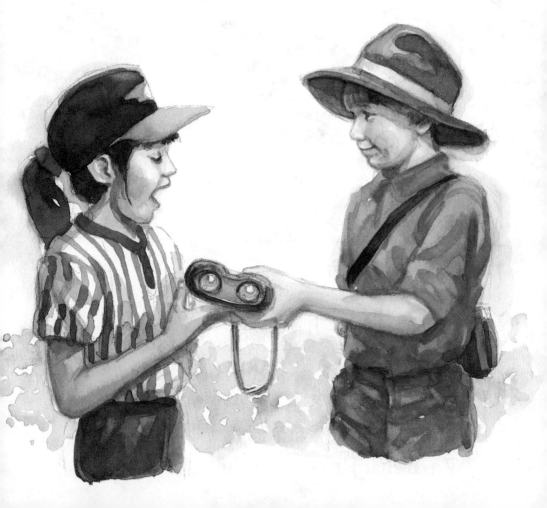

"Oh, I get it," said Maria.
"We are not spying on a jar
of *peanut butter*. We are spying on a
peanut butter jar filled with—"
"Money," said P.B. "My allowance, to be exact.

And this morning I noticed
something terrible!"
"What?" asked Mike.
"What?" asked Maria.
"My allowance has shrunk!" said P.B.
"Someone stole some of it!"
"A shrunken allowance! That *IS* terrible!"
said Maria.
"It sure is," said Mike.
"Tell us more, P.B."

Chapter Two: P.B.'s Story

"We have lots of empty peanut butter jars
in our garage," P.B. said. "They don't call me
P.B. for nothing! I love the stuff."
P.B. took a big bite
of his peanut butter sandwich.
He chewed and chewed.
Maria looked at her watch.
"Go on," she said.

P.B. went on with his story.
"I fill those jars with
rubber bands, paper clips,
candy, gum, rocks,
my crayons, my ants—"
Maria looked at her watch again.
"And my allowance," said P.B.

"How much allowance
do you get?" Mike asked.
"I get fifty cents a week," answered P.B.
"Wow!" said Mike. "That's more than I get."
"Not only that," said P.B. "I get more money
if I do extra chores."
P.B. unrolled a big chart.

MY ALLOWANCE
by P.B.

MONTH	WEEK #1	WEEK #2	WEEK #3	WEEK #4	WEEK #5	MONTHLY TOTAL
JUNE extra chores	50¢ <u>25¢</u> **75¢**	50¢ <u>15¢</u> **65¢**	50¢ <u>30¢</u> **80¢**	50¢ <u>15¢</u> **65¢**		**$2.85**
JULY extra chores	50¢ <u>15¢</u> **65¢**	50¢ <u>25¢</u> **75¢**	50¢ <u>5¢</u> **55¢**	50¢ <u>10¢</u> **60¢**	50¢ <u>$1.00</u> **$1.50**	**$4.05**
AUGUST extra chores	50¢ **50¢**	50¢ <u>10¢</u> **60¢**	50¢ <u>90¢</u> **$1.40**	50¢ <u>15¢</u> **65¢**		**$3.15**
					GRAND TOTAL	**$10.05**

"I began to save my money
on June 1," said P.B.
"I get paid every Saturday
in pennies, nickels, dimes, or quarters.
As you can see, my grand total
as of yesterday was ten dollars and five cents."
"Ten dollars and five cents!" said Maria.
"You're rich!"
"I work hard for my money,"
said P.B. "Very hard."

"How much is missing?" Mike asked.
"About an inch," P.B. said.
"An inch?" Maria asked. "Didn't you count it
this morning to see how much was missing?"

P.B. took another bite of his sandwich.
"I am too busy to count it today.
I have to spy. I have to catch the thief!
Anyway, I can see that my allowance has shrunk
with my very own eyes!"
"Look closely at my jar!"

"Yesterday the money filled the jar
to the top of the big *P*," P.B. said.
"Today the money fills the jar
only to the bottom of the big *P*.
My allowance has shrunk!"

Maria nodded her head.
"Let me see," said Mike.

"It has shrunk, all right," he said.
"But we should still count
the money to see how much is missing."

"We don't have time!" said Maria. "We are on
a very tight schedule!"
"We don't have time!" said P.B. "Because there
she is! There's the thief now!"

Chapter Three:
Some Important Questions

"Oh, no!" said P.B. "It can't be!
It's my sister Jill!"
"Let's sneak closer to the window!"
said Maria.
P.B., Mike, and Maria hid behind another tree.
Mike looked out.
"Jill is taking money from the jar!"
Mike said. "Now she is counting it.
Six quarters.
Three dimes.
Four nickels.
And two shiny pennies."
"Your allowance just shrunk
some more," said Maria.

"I can't believe it! My sister Jill!
Caught in the act!" P.B. said.
Just then, Jill came outside.
"I have an important question
for you, Jill," said P.B.
"Sure," said Jill. "Ask away."
"Did you take money
from my peanut butter jar just now?"
asked P.B.
"Yes, I did," said Jill.
"I needed change for video games
and for the gum machine.
I took two shiny pennies for my shoes."

"It was Jill who shrunk
your allowance, P.B.," said Mike.
"I didn't shrink P.B.'s allowance,"
Jill said.

"Yes, you did!" said Maria.
"We saw it shrink with our very own eyes."
"Take a closer look," said Jill.
P.B., Maria, and Mike
took a closer look at the jar.

"Look!" said P.B. "Jill is right!"
"She didn't really shrink my allowance!"
"I get it," said Maria.
"I don't," said Mike.
"Jill took six quarters,
three dimes, and four nickels," Maria said.
But she put two one dollar bills into the jar.
Two one dollar bills take up less space,
but they are worth the same as those coins."

"I also put back two old pennies
for the shiny ones in my shoes," said Jill.

"Thank you," said P.B. "Did you put back the money you took yesterday, too?"

"Yesterday?" asked Jill.

"Yes, yesterday," said P.B.

"I didn't take any money yesterday," said Jill. "I took money this afternoon. That was the only time."

"Then who took my money yesterday?" asked P.B.

"*That* is a very important question," said Maria.

"It sure is," said Mike.

Chapter Four: Too Late!

"Yesterday the money filled the jar
to the top of the big *P*," said P.B.
"This morning my allowance
was shrunken!"
"Yes, it was," said Mike.
"We saw it with our very own eyes!"
added Maria.
"Well, I did not take any of the
money," said Jill.
"We'll have to keep spying," said P.B.

Maria checked her watch.
"It is 12:25 P.M.
Mike and I have to leave for the park in five minutes."
Suddenly Jill pointed to the window.
"OH, NO!" she shouted.
"STOP THAT CAT!"

Too late!
The cat batted the peanut butter jar
with his paw.

The jar fell through the air.
Maria raced to catch it.
She jumped up.
She caught it!

"Hooray!" P.B. shouted. "Great catch!"

"Thanks," said Maria.

"You're really lucky!" said Jill.

"This time it didn't break."

"*This* time?" asked P.B.

"Have you seen the cat knock over my jar before today?"

"Well, yes," said Jill.

"Aha! It's the cat!" P.B. said.

"Is your cat the thief?" asked Mike.

"No," P.B. said. "But the mystery is solved."

"Really?" asked Mike.

"Yes. Tell us more, Jill," said P.B.

"Yesterday I saw the cat
knock your jar from the shelf," said Jill.
"Did the jar break?" asked P.B.
"Yes. It broke into many pieces,"
Jill answered slowly.
"Did you clean up the mess?" asked P.B.
"Of course," said Jill.
"Then I put your money
into another peanut butter jar," she added.

"A *bigger* jar, right?" asked P.B.
"Right," said Jill. "How did you know?"
"I'll explain. Follow me to the garage,
everybody!" said P.B.
"To the garage?" asked Mike.
"To the garage! Hurry!" shouted P.B.
"And bring the fruit punch."

Chapter Five: So Many Jars!

P.B., Mike, Maria, and Jill
ran to the garage.
"So many jars!" said Maria.
P.B. looked around.
"Just what I'm looking for!" he said.

He got two empty peanut butter jars.
One jar was bigger than the other.
"Give me the fruit punch," P.B. said to Mike.
P.B. poured some fruit punch into the smaller jar.
He poured the juice to the top of the big *P*.
"Watch this!" P.B. said.

He poured the same juice
into the bigger jar.
"Now the juice does not go
to the top of the big *P*," said Maria.
"The juice has shrunk!" said Mike.
"No," said Jill. "The juice has not shrunk."
"I get it," said Maria.
"I don't," said Mike.

"It is the same amount of juice," Maria said.
"It just looks like the juice has shrunk
because the jar is bigger."
"And that means my allowance
didn't shrink either!" said P.B.
"Right," Jill said. "We will find that out
when we count it."

Maria looked at her watch.
"It's 12:30 P.M.
It will take us fifteen minutes
to get to the park. We want to get there
in time for practice. We have no time
to count the money!"

"We can count the money
in five minutes," said Jill.
"And you can ride our bikes
to the park," said P.B.
"You will get there
in ten minutes that way."

"I'll count the quarters!" said Mike.
"I'll count the dimes!" said P.B.
"Okay, I'll count the nickels," said Maria.
"I'll count the pennies and the dollar bills," said Jill.
"Write down your answers here," said P.B.
Everybody counted the money.
"Now let's add it all up," said Jill.

"The grand total is ten dollars and five cents!" said Maria.

"Just like your chart!" said Mike.

"Hooray! Nothing is missing!" said P.B.

"Let's go!" said Maria.

Mike and Maria hopped on the bikes.

"Win that game!" shouted P.B.

"We will!" shouted Mike and Maria.

"P.B., may I ask you a question now?" said Jill.

"Ask away," said P.B.

"Why are you wearing that silly hat?"

"I'll tell you on the way to the park," said P.B.

• ABOUT THE ACTIVITIES •

When learning mathematics, it's important for children to have many opportunities to think, reason, and solve problems. Stories are ideal for this and *The Case of the Shrunken Allowance* presents a story that engages children's interest and gets them thinking about time, money, estimation, measurement, and logical reasoning.

This activity section revisits each chapter and gives your child suggestions for getting further involved with the mathematical ideas presented in the story. For all of the questions in the activities, encourage your child to explain his or her thinking behind the answers he or she gives. Listening to children's explanations is a way to gain understanding about the way they think. Be curious about how your child approaches the problems and how he or she reasons. Remember that there is no one best or right way to think about mathematical problems. Have fun with the math!

— Marilyn Burns

You'll find tips and suggestions for guiding the activities whenever you see a box like this!

RETELLING THE STORY

Look through the story again.

See if you can answer these questions.

Chapter One:

What does Maria mean when she says,

"We are on a tight schedule"?

Chapter Two:

Why does P.B. think someone stole his allowance?

Chapter Three:

Count up the coins Jill took from the jar.

Is this the same as what she put in the jar?

Chapter Four:

Why did P.B. think that Jill had put the

money in a bigger jar?

Chapter Five:

Jill says, "The juice has not shrunk."

Can you explain why she is right?

Keeping Time

Maria knew how long it would take her and Mike to eat lunch, walk to the park, practice hitting balls, and then win their game. How good are you at estimating how much time it takes to do some of the things you do? Make guesses about how many minutes it takes you to do each of the things below. Then keep time the next chance you have.

What I Do	My Estimate	My Time
Brush Teeth		
Eat Breakfast		
Go from home to school		
Clean room		

Try estimating and timing other things that you do.

Ways to Make 50¢

How many different ways do you think there are for P.B. to get his fifty-cent allowance? Find as many as you can. Hint: You may want to make a chart like this to keep track of the different ways:

quarters	dimes	nickels	pennies
2			
	5		
1	2		5

There are almost 50 ways to show 50 cents with different coins. Your child may need to use actual money to do this figuring. He or she also most likely won't be interested in finding all of the solutions. That's fine. It's also fine for children this age to look for different possibilities by searching randomly.

Math in the Kitchen Sink

Find five to eight empty containers that are different sizes. Line them up in order from the one you think holds the least amount to the one that you think holds the most. Then use water to test if you lined them up right: fill the jar you think is the smallest; then pour the water into the next size jar. If the water doesn't fill it, the next jar really is larger. If the water spills over, you have the jars in the wrong order.

More Math in the Kitchen Sink

Use the smallest jar or container you found and fill it with water. Choose another jar or container and, with a crayon, marker, or piece of masking tape, mark how high you think it will be filled when you pour in the water from the smallest jar or container. Then pour in the water and see how close you were. Do the same for the other jars.

A Hard Problem

When they counted the money, Mike counted the quarters, P.B. counted the dimes, Maria counted the nickels, and Jill counted the pennies and dollar bills. It all added up to $10.05.

How many quarters, dimes, nickels, pennies, and dollar bills could they have counted to add up to $10.05?

Many different possible combinations of coins and dollar bills add up to $10.05. Your child may need to use actual money to do this figuring. If this problem is too hard, model a correct solution and have your child count the money along with you.